Maybe Wanda will let us stay for dinner?

There are even homemade chocolate-chip
cookies for dessert!
Lunchtime is going to be my favorite class.

Gobble, gobble, munch, munch.
Look out, stomach, here comes lunch!
Hey, these taste great!
Maybe I'll get three more.

They smell good if you take your hand off your nose.
I'm going to get two!

Hey! Wanda doesn't look so bad.
And look! She made hamburgers and french fries.

We're through the door.
We get our trays.
They don't even offer us blindfolds.

I'll bet Wanda's stirring up poisonous pots
full of molten messes of steamy slime.

We're being lined up and marched
down to the *cafetorium*.

Uh-oh, it's time for lunch!
I'm too young to die.
Can't we have a math test instead?
Isn't it time for vaccinations?

I hope the spaghetti will make good shoelaces.

and the spinach is great for vinyl repairs.

the pudding will stick to anything...

the mashed potatoes are good for sculpting...

Even if you can't eat the food, they say
it's always good for something.
The meatballs are aerodynamic...

For dessert we might have ton cake,
which is pound cake . . .

only heavier.

SOUFFLÉ OF SCIENCE EXPERIMENTS
and TOXIC WASTE TACOS

CAUTION
TOXIC
WASTE

I wonder what Wanda's cooking up right now?
Today's menu will probably be:

ROADKILL RAVIOLI

SPAGHETTI WITH BOWLING BALLS

I heard she doesn't throw *anything* away!

We've heard Wanda's into recycling.
The water she washes the dishes in will be . . .

tomorrow's soup of the day.

gooey ghouls in her *goulash*...

real sand and witches in her sandwiches.

sweaty socks in her *moussaka*...

All the kids say that Wanda uses natural ingredients
in her dishes: organic rats in her *ratatouille*...

The kids made sure to check the specials the next day.

And when class pets disappeared...

Derek says that at Wanda's old school, kids found sneakers and baseball caps in her tuna surprise.

Freddy heard that she learned to cook on a pirate ship, so don't go near the kitchen.

Eric says that instead of a car, she drives a garbage truck to school.

We got a new cafeteria lady today.
Her name is Wanda Belch.

For Jo Small, my sister,
with love
—M.T.

To Spanky and Little Din
—J.L.

Library of Congress Catalog Card Number: 97-61899
ISBN 0-590-50493-2
Text copyright © 1998 by Mike Thaler.
Illustrations copyright © 1998 by Jared D. Lee Studio, Inc.
All rights reserved. Published by Scholastic Inc.

10 9 8 7 6

Printed in the U.S.A.

First printing, September 1998

0/0 01 02

24

The Cafeteria Lady
from the
Black Lagoon

by Mike Thaler · pictures by Jared Lee

SCHOLASTIC INC.

New York Toronto London Auckland Sydney